5059

JP   Stinson, Kathy.
Stins   Steven's baseball mitt : a book about being adopted /
          story by Kathy Stinson ; art by Robin Baird Lewis. --
          Toronto : Annick Press, c1992.
            1 v. (unpaged) : ill.

          06291880   ISBN:1550372335 (lib. bdg.)

          1. Adoption - Fiction. I. Lewis, Robin Baird. II. Title

     7301   92APR22   06/se   1-00991760

Steven's Baseball Mitt

A Book About Being Adopted

Story by
Kathy Stinson

Art by
Robin Baird Lewis

ANNICK PRESS

© 1992 Kathy Stinson (text)
© 1992 Robin Baird Lewis (art)

Design and graphic realization by Robin Baird Lewis

Annick Press Ltd.

Annick Press gratefully acknowledges the support of The Canada Council and the Ontario Arts Council

Canadian Cataloguing in Publication Data

Stinson, Kathy
   Steven's baseball mitt

ISBN 1-55037-233-5 (bound)   ISBN 1-55037-232-7 (ptk.)

1. Adoption — Juvenile fiction.   2. Picture-books
for children.   I. Lewis, Robin Baird,   II. Title.

PS8587.T56S7 1992   JC813′ .54   C91-095480-1
PZ7.S75St 1992

Distribution for Canada and the U.S.A.:
Firefly Books Ltd.
250 Sparks Avenue
North York, Ontario
M2H 2S4   Canada

Printed and bound in Canada
by D.W. Friesen & Sons

Typeset by Justified Type Inc., Guelph

 Printed on acid free paper

K.S.—
Dedicated with thanks to
Keith, Roslyn, Tim, Scott, Nell, Megan, Omar, Andrea, and Percy,
but above all to Heather
who led me to their stories

R.B.L.—
for my parents, Georgie and Reginald, co-founders of a creative brood,
for their years of love, support and defy-the-odds encouragement;
and to

I feel different.
Because I am adopted.

Sometimes I feel different
good. Because I know my
parents really wanted me.

But when Jason says, "Why didn't your real mom want you?"
I feel different bad.

To me
my mom is
my real mom.
She takes me
to the dentist

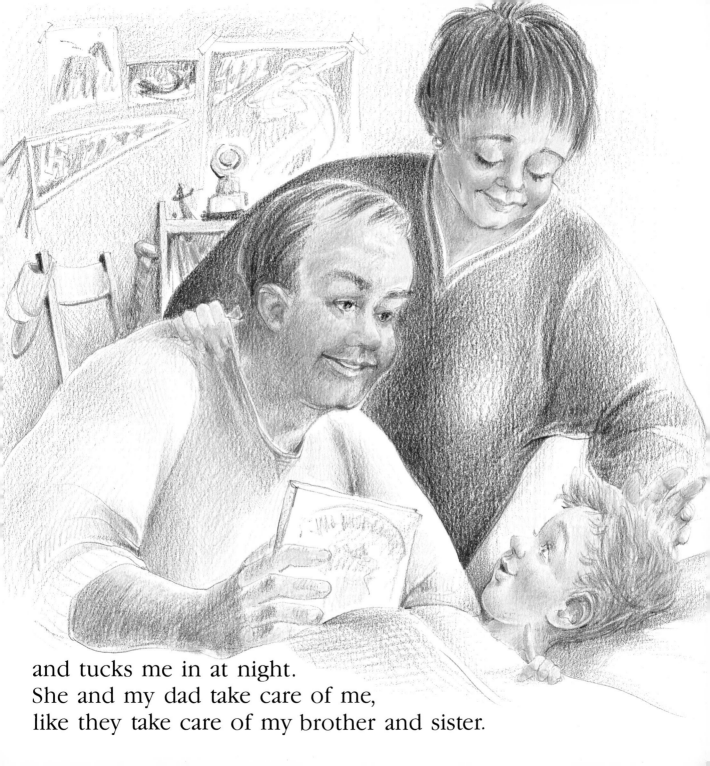

and tucks me in at night.
She and my dad take care of me,
like they take care of my brother and sister.

But Jason means my birth mother, the one who had me inside her before I was born.

I don't know
anything
about her.

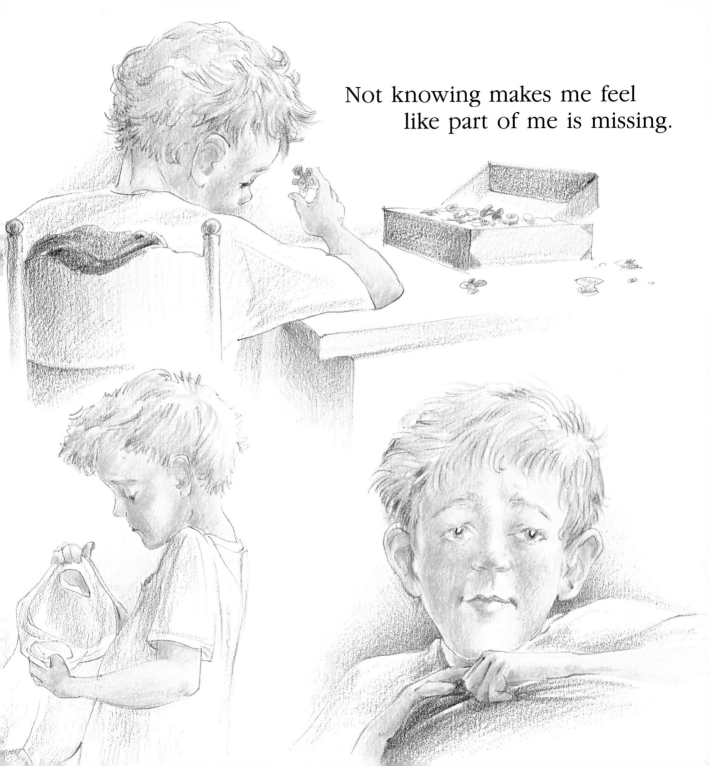

Not knowing makes me feel
like part of me is missing.

Sometimes I wonder
what she's like.
Does she have
curly hair like me?

Would she make me
clean my room?

Maybe she lives in a mansion with a swimming pool and a skating rink in the backyard and a video arcade in the rec room.

Maybe she's famous.

But mostly I think she was a teenager who wouldn't be able to take care of me very well, no matter how much she wanted to.

My mom says that giving me up for adoption was the most loving thing my birth mother could do.

So how come thinking about her sometimes makes me so mad?

I wonder if my birth mother
ever thinks about me.
On my birthday especially,
I wonder if she's sad or happy.

Once I got worried thinking
about my birth mother.
What if she really
did want me?

What if my mom just took
me because she wanted
a baby so much?

Thinking about that
    gave me bad dreams.

Then my parents told me again how I came to be part of this family. After my brother and sister, my parents couldn't have any more children.

They talked to some people who knew about babies that needed a family to grow up in.

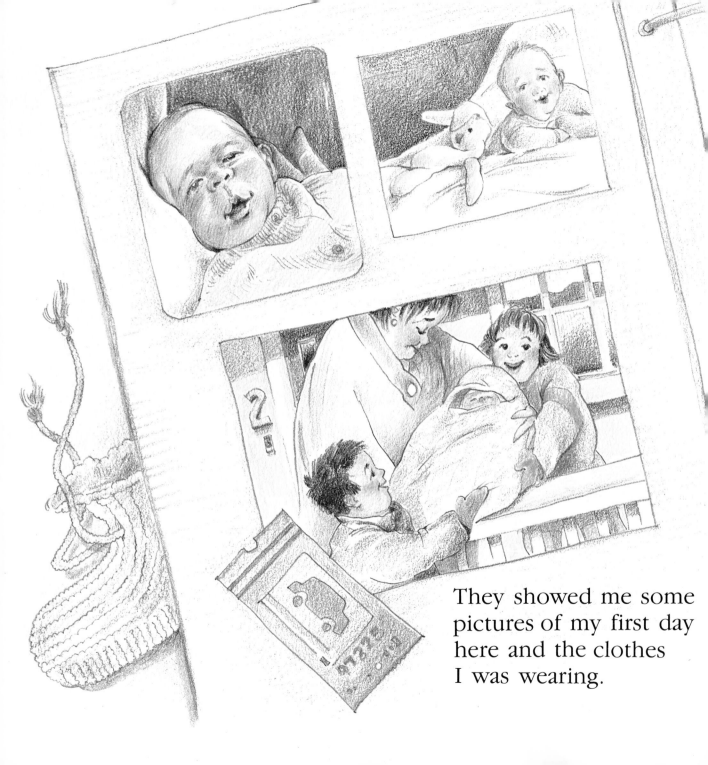

They showed me some
pictures of my first day
here and the clothes
I was wearing.

My mom also said when I'm older she could help me find my birth mother. Or maybe just find out more about her.

So I guess she must not have stolen me.

But I still sometimes wonder if it would hurt my mom's feelings if I wanted to find out about my birth mother.

I might like to find her some day, but I would never want to go live with her.

I can't imagine belonging with another family. Even if the other people looked more like me.

Because this is my family.
This is where I belong.

Other Annick books by Kathy Stinson

Red Is Best
Big Or Little?
The Bare Naked Book
The Dressed Up Book
Those Green Things
Teddy Rabbit
Mom and Dad Don't Live Together Any More